Phonetic Storybook 11

The
Owl
Book

by Sue Dickson

Illustrated by Norma Portadino

Total Language Arts K-3
Reading•Writing•Spelling•Phonics•Speaking

Sing, Spell
Read & Write

Copyright 1978, Sue Dickson, Extended University, CBN University
Virginia Beach, VA 23463.

Contents

Bozo
the Clown
Comes
to Town

Vocabulary

1. chow
2. shower
3. towel
4. town
5. now
6. down
7. brown
8. flower
9. flowers
10. cow
11. Howard

12. owl
13. wow
14. clown
15. frown
16. bow
17. bowed
18. howl
19. howled
20. gown

21. uncle

3

Andy jumped from his bed and ran to take a shower. Then he dried with his towel and ran to get dressed.

Today was Andy's big day. The circus had come to town at last !

"Hurry down to eat," yelled Mom. "It's nine o'clock now. We must be in town by ten. Uncle Howard will meet us at the big tent."

"I like the flowers in your dress, Mom. You look pretty," Andy said.

"You look fine in your brown shirt, too, Andy," said Mom.

6

Andy ate his eggs. Then Mom said, "Andy, go open the gate for Brown Cow. She can go to eat grass on the hill. I will feed Lassie some dog chow. Then we will go."

7

When Andy came back,
he asked, "Now can we go?
I can't wait to see the
circus !"

"Yes, now it is time to
go," said Mom.

Uncle Howard met Mom and Andy at the big tent. Andy looked way up to the top. "Wow !" cried Andy.

"It **is** big," said Uncle Howard. "Now come with me, Andy. We will go to see Bozo the Clown get dressed."

9

Uncle Howard
and Bozo
were pals.

"Hi, Andy,"
said Bozo.
"Would you
like to see me paint my face?"

"Wow ! Yes !" said Andy.

Bozo the Clown put thick
white cream on his face.

Then he painted fat red lips.

Next, he put a big red spot on each cheek.

"Now what is missing?" said Bozo with a frown.

"Your big red nose !" said Andy.

Bozo put on his huge red nose, and bowed to Andy. Andy just howled !

12

Then Bozo and Uncle Howard, Mom and Andy rushed to the big tent.

"We must not miss the first act," cried Andy.

"And I must not miss my big act," said Bozo. "I will wave to you, Andy. Have fun at the circus today."

13

Andy liked
all the clowns
best...

Fat clowns, skinny clowns,
red clowns and brown.

One in a funny gown,
up-side down !

A clown with
an owl...

A clown with
a flower...

A clown in a bath-tub
taking a shower !

A clown that
 could howl...
A clown with
 a cow...

And best of all, **Bozo,** taking a bow !

The End

A
Brownie
Scout
at Joan's House

Vocabulary

1. house
2. scout
3. scouts
4. sound
5. sounds
6. proud
7. around
8. shout
9. shouted
10. flour
11. about
12. couch

13. scouting
14. ground
15. bounce
16. found
17. our
18. loud

fin ish
finish
19. finished

pā per
20. paper
21. says (sez)

20

Joan ran into the house.
"**Mommy !**" she shouted.
"Look at this paper.
My teacher gave it to me.
It says that I may be a
Brownie Scout !"

"Lots of the girls in my class will be Scouts," Joan went on. "I can't wait!"

"That sounds like fun," said Mother. "We can go see the Brownie Scout Leader. This paper tells me that Miss Proud will be the Leader."

"She lives just around the corner," shouted Joan. "Let's go see her now!"

Mother said, "First, I need to finish this pie crust. And I must wipe the flour off my hands, Joan. Then we will go."

When Mom had finished, she and Joan went to see Miss Proud.

"We would like to find out about Brownie Scouts," said Joan.

Miss Proud said, "Come in the house. We can sit here on my couch.

24

Miss Proud then told Mom and Joan about scouting. She said, "We will go on a camp-out. We will sleep on the ground in tents. Do you have a sleeping bag, Joan?" she asked.

25

"Yes," said Joan. "Daddy
has a sleeping bag. He was
a scout."

Joan was so happy, she
began to bounce up and
down on the couch.

"Sit still, Joan," said Mom.
"I'm glad we found out about
scouts. It sounds like fun !"

"We must go now," said Mom. "It has been about an hour, and I have a pie in the oven."

Joan gave a loud shout. "YIPPEE !" she said. "I am going to be a Brownie Scout !"

The End 27

The Snowman

Vocabulary

1. snow
2. snowing
    snow man
3. snowman
4. low
5. slow
6. throw

7. crow
8. row
9. grow
10. bow
11. window
12. show
13. blow
14. snow ball

It was the first snow of the winter. Ted, Karen and Liz ran out to make a big snowman.

"The north wind doth blow, and we shall have snow...and a snowman," said Daddy. He was looking out the window at the children.

"Come see the fine show, Mother," he said.

"Look, here is a carrot for his nose," said Ted.

"And two black coals so he can see," said Karen.

"Let's put this bow tie on his neck," said Liz.

31

Dad said,
"Let's get
a hat for
the snowman,
Mom.
We can go
out and help
finish him."

"You will never grow up,"
Mom said. "Let's go! We
can throw some snowballs
too!"

"O.K. Mom, not so slow!"
said Dad. And out they went.

Mom put
the hat on
the snowman.

"Look, Dad! We put
stones in a row for his
buttons," said Liz.

"And I'll put this pipe
in his mouth," said Dad.

"Now **there** is a snowman to crow about!" said Dad.

"Let's go in for some hot chocolate," said Mom.

"Yes," said Dad. "We can see our snowman from the window. If it keeps on snowing, we may see him grow!"

The End

The
New Crew

Vocabulary

1. few
2. flew
3. mew
4. threw
5. new

6. crew
7. screw
8. screws
9. stew
10. chew

35

Bobby and Steve lived near a pond.

"Let's make a raft to sail on this pond," said Steve.

"Yes," said Bobby. "We can get some logs at my house."

"I will get a hammer and nails and screws," said Steve.

"Wait," said Bobby," I must go home to eat now. I will meet you after lunch."

"O.K.," said Steve.

"Don't chew the stew so fast, Bobby," said his mom. "What is the rush?"

"Steve and I are going to make a raft. We will sail it on the pond. We will be the crew," said Bobby.

"That will be fun," said Mom. "How about a few cookies and some gum to chew? I will put them in a bag for you and Steve. You can eat them as you make the raft."

"Thank you, Mom," said Bobby, and off he flew to meet Steve.

On his way
Bobby met Willy,
his big cat.

"Mew, mew," went Willy.

"Would you like to come
with me, Willy?" asked Bobby.
Willy rubbed Bobby's leg.

Bobby and Steve began the
raft. Hammers and nails flew!

At last the
raft was finished.

It even had a sail
on a mast !

Just as
Steve
and
Bobby
threw the raft into the pond,
a bird flew by. He flew up
to sit on the mast !

All at once,

lots of things

happened! Willy jumped onto the raft to get that bird! As he jumped, a big puff of wind blew on the sail! The rope flew out of Steve's hand...and **away went the raft** across the pond!

"Look at the new crew!"
yelled Bobby and Steve. They
both giggled and giggled at
such a funny thing !

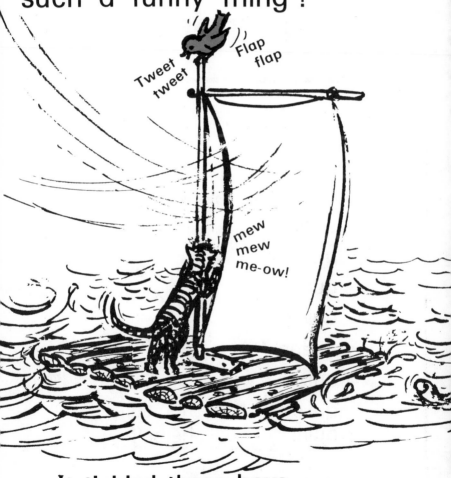

It tickled those boys.
Would it tickle you
to see this new and funny crew?

The End 43

qu

Quite
a
Surprise

Vocabulary

1. quite
2. question
3. queer
4. quilt
5. quit
6. quick
7. queen
8. quiz

qui̅et
9. quiet

do ing
10. doing

al ways
11. always

go ing
12. going

her self
13. herself

Jean was so quiet !

Mom asked, "What are you doing, Jean? And what are those little scraps of cloth?"

Jean was sorry her mom
had asked that question.
She had hoped to have a
surprise for her.

"I am going
to make
something
for you,"
said Jean.

She hoped that Mom
would not quiz her more.

Then Mom gave Jean a
queer look and said,"I hope
it will not be a dress !"
They both giggled.

Jean was making a quilt for Mom. She would have to quit when Mom's quick steps came near.

"I must get this quilt finished on time." said Jean to herself.

On Mother's birthday, Jean's surprise was finished.

"A quilt !" Mother cried when she saw it. "It is so pretty ! This is quite a surprise. Even a queen would love this quilt, Jean !"

"You <u>are</u> my queen, Mom !" said Jean.

48

Mom gave Jean a big hug.
"Thank you, Jean," she
said. "I will always see your
love in each little stitch of
that quilt ! Thank you for a
very happy birthday !"

The End   49

The
New
White Car

Vocabulary

1. white
2. which
3. where
4. when
5. wheel
6. wheels
7. wheat
8. Wheaties
9. whiz

10. what
11. whipped
12. whopper
13. while

a while
14. awhile

15. signs
16. who

The Millers have a new
white car. They are going
on a trip in it.

Mom
is going to look at the map
to see which roads to take.

51

Dad will drive for awhile.

Sam
and Frank
will look at
the road signs,
so they can tell
where they are
and when to turn.

"I just love this new steering wheel," said Dad.

"What is that growing over there?" asked Frank.

"That is wheat," said Dad.

Mom asked, "Who can tell me what is made from wheat?"

"Wheaties!" yelled Frank.

"What else?" asked Mom.

"Hamburger rolls," Dad said. "Shall we stop at the next hamburger place we see?"

"Look at that sign," said Sam. "I can read it. W-H-I-Z, WHIZ INN !"

"I see it," said Frank. "Hamburgers. Soda. Let's whiz in there, Dad."

"It looks like a nice place," said Mom. "Yes, let's whiz in there."

''See their flag whipping in the wind,'' said Sam.

Dad drove in
and stopped the car.
The Miller family got out.

"When we come back out,
it will be Mom's turn to drive
our new car," said Dad.

"Good!" said Mom.
"That will be fun."

The End

Where is that
popsicle man?

Where is his
white truck with
the red wheels?

What will you
buy when he
64 comes?

I want a
whipped cream
whopper!

The End